The Emperor's New Clothes

Kaye Umansky

Illustrated by Caroline Crossland

A & C BLACK • LONDON

Contents

A Letter from the Playwright

The story of *The Emperor's New Clothes* has always been a favourite of mine, and I have had enormous fun turning it into a play. The story touches on many themes – vanity, pomposity, the disparity between rich and poor, and so on – all of which makes it interesting. But above all, it's funny. Most of us have dreamt at some time or other about standing at a bus stop or on a stage – and suddenly realising we have no clothes on. The experience is one we all subconsciously dread. That's why it's so hilarious when it happens to someone else. As Mel Brooks once said: "Tragedy is when I cut my finger. Comedy is when you fall into an open sewer and die."

The story lends itself very well to dramatisation. The central character is a fashion victim, which holds out all sorts of possibilities for wild experimentation with costume. Having the 'right' clothes is very much a contemporary concern. Young people agonise over trainers in much the same way as the Emperor loses sleep over the appropriate outfit to wear in the forthcoming Grand Parade.

The play is intended to be funny, so the cast will need a strong sense of humour. There are ten main speaking parts and ten smaller parts. There are two Footmen, who never speak but are nonetheless required to do quite a bit of acting! You can include a great number of children as Townsfolk and Urchins if you are looking for ways to expand the number of parts. They will become members of the crowd and all get the chance to say some lines in chorus.

Another way of creating further parts for dancers would be to include a country dance during one of the scenes set in the Market Place.

The Director's Notes at the back of this book are intended to help you. However, do not feel duty bound to follow them to the letter. You may well have better ideas yourself. The same applies to the script. Feel free to add bits, cut, change or adapt. If you want to include more songs or dances or jokes containing topical references to the school, do so.

If you intend using this play as a reading exercise in the classroom, some preparation beforehand would help you to reap rewards. At first, children won't know how to read a playscript, as reading dialogue is so different to reading a story. Each character has an individual voice and a personality which must be maintained throughout. Spend some time discussing characterisation, pace and timing with the children before you begin.

However you use the play, whether to read it in class or put on a full-scale performance on stage, I hope you have a lot of fun with it. I certainly did.

Characters In Order Of Appearance

The Towncriers: Crier One

Crier Two

Bogus

Fishweedle

Gert the Washerwoman

Walter the Woodcutter

The Emperor

The Prime Minister

The Footmen: Footman One

Footman Two

The Empress

The Imperial Mum

The Tradespeople: The Flower Seller

The Fruit Seller

The Ribbon Seller

The Milkmaid

The Pie Man

The Blind Beggar

The Shoeshine Boy

The Townsfolk

The Urchins

List of Scenes and their Locations

Prologue – An Introduction : *The Wood*

Act 1

Scene 1 – The Honeyed Tongue : *The Wood*

Scene 2 – Talk About Vain! : *The Emperor's Chambers*

Scene 3 – Down With The Emperor! : *The Market Place*

Scene 4 – He's Gotta Have It! : *The Emperor's Chambers*

[Interval if desired]

Act 2

Scene 1 – This Is The Life! : *The Weaving Room*

Scene 2 – Time To View : *The Emperor's Chambers*

Scene 3 – The Cloth Revealed : *The Weaving Room*

Scene 4 – Ooh! He's Got No Clothes On! : *The Market Place*

The playing time is approximately 50 minutes without an interval.

Prologue – An Introduction

The Wood. There is a tree stump for sitting on. Enter the TOWNCRIERS at the back of the hall. They parade through the audience. CRIER ONE shouts "Oyez! Oyez!" through a megaphone. CRIER TWO rings a bell and carries a large rolled-up scroll. They come to stand at the front of the stage.

CRIER ONE: Oyez! Oyez! Pray, gather round
         And pin your ears back well!

CRIER TWO: Sit up! Sit straight! And <u>listen</u>!
         For a tale we have to tell.

(CRIER TWO rings his bell.)

CRIER ONE: A tale of foolish vanity,
         Of craftiness and guile.

CRIER TWO: We hope it makes you tremble
         And we hope it makes you smile.

(CRIER TWO rings his bell again.)

CRIER ONE: *(in a normal voice)* What are you doing?

CRIER TWO: Ringing my bell after my line. Like it says in the script.

CRIER ONE: Well, don't. It does my head in. Miss it out.

CRIER TWO: Can't do that. Got to stick to the script. Here it is, look.

(He takes a piece of paper from his pocket and shows it to CRIER ONE.)

CRIER TWO: "Rings bell." See? So I'm ringing it. *(He does so once more.)*

CRIER ONE: Will you <u>stop</u> that? Just because we're town criers, it doesn't all have to be noise and shouting. We can explain about things and set the scene nice and quietly <u>without</u> a bell.

CRIER TWO: It won't sound so good.

CRIER ONE: It'll sound great. Trust me. Ready for the last verse? But no bell. Agreed?

CRIER TWO: *(with a sigh)* No bell.

CRIERS ONE & TWO: We've stood too long upon this stage
And now we're going away.
The time has come – so settle back
And Let's Begin The Play!

*(We hear a drum roll from off stage. Ceremoniously, they unroll the scroll. On it, in very large letters are the words: **THE EMPEROR'S NEW CLOTHES**.)*

CRIERS ONE & TWO: The Emperor's New Clothes!

(The TOWNCRIERS sing the following song to the tune of 'John Brown's Body'.)

HE KEEPS ON BUYING CLOTHES

1. A hundred pairs of trousers and a hundred pairs of shoes,
    A hundred silk kimonos in a hundred different hues,
    A new pair of pyjamas every time he takes a snooze –
    But he keeps on buying clothes!

    That's the trouble with the Emperor!
    That's the trouble with the Emperor!
    That's the trouble with the Emperor!
    He keeps on buying clothes!

2. He throws around his money like a multi-millionaire,
    His wardrobe's simply bursting and there's not an inch to spare,
    And yet he's always moaning he ain't got a thing to wear –
    So he keeps on buying clothes!

    That's the trouble with the Emperor!
    That's the trouble with the Emperor!
    That's the trouble with the Emperor!
    He keeps on buying clothes!

(The TOWNCRIERS exit.)

Act 1, Scene 1 – The Honeyed Tongue

The Wood. Enter BOGUS and FISHWEEDLE at a run. They are wearing convicts' clothes and are carrying large balls attached to their feet by chains.

BOGUS:

That's it! I've had it! I've got to sit down!
(He collapses onto the tree stump.)
I'm not moving another inch with this ball and chain attached to my foot. *(He rubs his ankle.)*
Ouch. An axe, that's what we need. Go and get us an axe, Fishweedle.

FISHWEEDLE:

So where am I supposed to get an axe from?

BOGUS:

Isn't it obvious? Find a simple woodman and persuade him to give you one.

FISHWEEDLE:

Ah, come on, Bogus. In these clothes?

BOGUS:

What have I always said to you? It's not the looks that count. It's the honeyed tongue. What are we, Fishweedle?

FISHWEEDLE:

Con men?

BOGUS:

Wrong. We are con-<u>artistes</u>. Bogus and Fishweedle, Kings of the Confidence Trick. We are smooth. We are smart. We are <u>foxy</u>!

FISHWEEDLE:

Then how come we spent the last ten years in the nick for forgery?

BOGUS:

Because, Fishweedle, we didn't get the chance to speak in court. Two minutes, that's all I needed, and my honeyed tongue would have had that jury all wrapped up...

FISHWEEDLE:

Ssssh!

BOGUS:

What?

FISHWEEDLE:

Someone's coming. Hide!

(They hide behind a tree. Enter GERT THE WASHERWOMAN with a basket, humming happily. She sits on the tree stump and takes an apple from her pocket.)

BOGUS: What d'you think?

FISHWEEDLE: Worth a try.

(They step out from behind the tree. GERT freezes, apple halfway to her mouth.)

BOGUS: Good morning, madam, my o my what a wonderful day. We'd like to introduce ourselves, we're strangers to the area, my name's Bogus and this here's my good friend and colleague Fishweedle...

GERT: *(lets out a high pitched scream)* AAAAAAAAAAH!

BOGUS: Now, now, no need to be alarmed...

GERT: *(screaming more loudly)* AAAAAAAAAAAAAH!

(GERT takes a variety of things from her basket – a whistle, a football rattle, a hooter. She uses them all and screams again.)

GERT: *(even more loudly)* AAAAAAHHHHHH!

(Enter WALTER THE WOODCUTTER at a run, wildly brandishing his axe.)

WALTER: I'm comin', I'm comin'! Get behind me, Gert, I'll save yer!

BOGUS: *(backing off)* Whoa! Whoa! Hold your horses, friend!

WALTER: Stay right where you are, you nasty escaped convicts, you!

GERT: You tell 'em, Walter.

BOGUS: Nasty escaped con... Oh! I get it! It's the suits, right? *(He bursts into laughter.)* Imagine, Fishweedle! They think the suits are real! *(He nudges FISHWEEDLE who obligingly joins in the laughter.)*

FISHWEEDLE: Ha, ha, ha, ha, ha!

WALTER:	What are you on about? What's so funny?
BOGUS:	You've mistaken our costumes for the real thing.
GERT:	Costumes?
BOGUS:	Yes. Our costumes for the play.
GERT:	Play? You mean – you're play actors?
BOGUS:	Of course. A couple of innocent strolling players, bringing culture to the masses. Our latest production is a prison drama. It's a bleak, hard hitting account of life behind bars.
FISHWEEDLE:	It's called "Banged Up And Desperate".
BOGUS:	Give the lady one of our playbills, Fishweedle.
FISHWEEDLE:	Certainly. *(He pats his pockets, then lets out a deep sigh.)* Well, blow me if I haven't left them on the kitchen table.
BOGUS:	You haven't! Oh, Fishweedle, you old silly billy. How are we going to advertise our play?
GERT:	Don't worry. Don't sound like our kind of show, does it, Walter?
FISHWEEDLE:	Understandable. It's not everyone's cup of tea.
GERT:	I likes a bit of a laugh meself. Bit of a sing-song.
BOGUS:	Don't we all?
FISHWEEDLE:	Where would we be without a bit of a laugh, I always say.
WALTER:	*(puzzled)* I don't get it. Ain't they escaped convicts, then?
GERT:	'Course not, you silly old fool. These gentlemen are actors. *(To BOGUS & FISHWEEDLE)* He's a bit slow on the uptake.

(BOGUS and FISHWEEDLE exchange a private wink.)

BOGUS: Nice sharp axe you have there, Walter. Not up to slicing through metal, of course, but a fine axe for all that.

WALTER: Yes it is.

BOGUS: Yes what is?

WALTER: Me axe. It's up to slicin' through metal.

BOGUS: Three pennies says it isn't.

WALTER: Six says it is.

BOGUS: You're on. Now, how are we going to settle this? I know! Let's see if it'll slice through the chains on my feet. I'll put my foot – like so, and Walter, you do your worst. I hope you're good at aiming, ha ha... Ooer... *(He covers his eyes.)*

(WALTER spits on his hands, readies himself, brings the axe down and cuts through the chain. FISHWEEDLE pointedly looks the other way.)

BOGUS: Well, I'm blowed. Look at that, Fishweedle.

FISHWEEDLE: What? I didn't see.

BOGUS: Deary me, has the poor man got to do it all again? Sorry, Walter, my friend seems to have doubts. Would you mind?

(WALTER obliges and cuts through FISHWEEDLE's chain.)

FISHWEEDLE: Well, bless my soul. That's some axe you've got there, Walter. Easy as slicing through paper.

WALTER: Yeah. Where's me sixpence?

BOGUS: Pay the man, Fishweedle.

FISHWEEDLE: I thought you had the purse.

BOGUS: No. I thought you did.

FISHWEEDLE:	Must have left it on the kitchen table, along with the handbills. What a featherbrain I am, ha, ha, ha.
BOGUS:	*(ruefully)* Us creative actor types, eh? And I'll tell you something else we forgot! The sandwiches!
FISHWEEDLE:	Oh, no! Not the sandwiches!
WALTER:	Never mind the sandwiches. What about me money?
GERT:	Walter! Will you stop that! I'm sorry, gentlemen, he's that stubborn. Tell you what. Why don't you come along back to the cottage for a cup of tea and a bite to eat? It'll help make up for all the misunderstanding.
BOGUS:	Well, if you're sure it's no trouble...
GERT:	No trouble at all. You can meet my old dad. He's a weaver.
BOGUS:	<u>Really</u>? A <u>weaver</u>, eh? Hear that, Fishweedle? Gert's old dad is a <u>weaver</u>...

(ALL exit, talking as they go.)

Act 1, Scene 2 – Talk About Vain!

The Emperor's Chambers. Lights up on an elaborate throne, a coat stand draped with dazzling outfits and a full length mirror. All the actors are very still, as if frozen. The EMPEROR poses before the mirror; the PRIME MINISTER is grovelling to him. The two FOOTMEN stand expressionless in the background. The actors remain motionless throughout the TOWNCRIERS' exchange.

Enter the TOWNCRIERS, one carrying a scroll. They position themselves at the front of the stage.

CRIER ONE:	*(out of the corner of his mouth)* No bell, right?
CRIER TWO:	All right, all right.
CRIER ONE:	Yes, here we are. We're back again All bushy-tailed and keen.

CRIER TWO:	Our task? To introduce you To the next enthralling scene.
CRIER ONE:	Prepare now for the Emperor. An empty-headed ass...
CRIER TWO:	Who spends long hours posturing Before a looking glass,
CRIER ONE:	Indulging in his one and only All consuming passion
CRIER TWO:	Trying on and posing in The very latest fashion.

*(They unroll a new scroll which reads: **TALK ABOUT VAIN!**)*

CRIERS ONE & TWO:	Talk About Vain!

(They exit. The EMPEROR starts primping in front of the mirror.)

EMPEROR:	So, Prime Minister. What do you think of the new suit? It's for the Grand Parade.
PRIME MINISTER:	Your Majesty, what can I say? It's bold – yet subtle. It's classic – yet excitingly different. It's traditional – and yet it's now!
EMPEROR:	I had it specially shipped in. It's by the famous Vulgarian designer, you know. Otto Hoot.
PRIME MINISTER:	I knew it. I took one look, sire, and I said to myself, that suit is a Hoot.
EMPEROR:	You think pink's my colour, then?
PRIME MINISTER:	Oh, I do! You look lovely in it, Your Wonderfulness.
EMPEROR:	Hmm. Even so, I must say I'm a little disappointed. I don't feel it <u>sparkles</u> enough. Perhaps I'll wear the red after all.
PRIME MINISTER:	*(to FOOTMAN ONE)* The red, man, the red!

(FOOTMAN ONE takes a red costume off the stand and gives it to the EMPEROR.)

EMPEROR: *(holding it against himself)* Hmm. Of course, blue is really my colour.

(He drops the red outfit on the floor. FOOTMAN ONE retrieves it.)

PRIME MINISTER: The blue, the blue!

(FOOTMAN TWO passes the EMPEROR a blue costume. He holds it up.)

EMPEROR: The trouble is, I wore blue last year.

PRIME MINISTER: Ah.

(The EMPEROR drops the blue outfit on the floor. FOOTMAN TWO retrieves it.)

EMPEROR: And this <u>is</u> a Hoot. His name is on everyone's lips.

PRIME MINISTER: And you can carry it off, sire.

EMPEROR: Yes. But is it eye-catching enough? I like to put on a good show. My loyal subjects look to their Emperor to bring a bit of glamour into their squalid little lives.

PRIME MINISTER: And you do, sire, you do. The Emperor's Grand Parade is the high spot of their humdrum year.

EMPEROR: I know. You know, Prime Minister, poor people always look so dreary. No flair at all. I dread to think what they'd spend money on. If they had any.

PRIME MINISTER: Dull, practical things, I expect, sire. Clogs. Sensible coats. Flat caps. Ill-fitting tank tops...

EMPEROR: Exactly. Anyway, I've decided. I <u>shall</u> wear this in the Grand Parade. But I shall add some extra ribbons. To jazz it up a bit.

(Enter the EMPRESS with lots of bags. She drapes them over the FOOTMEN.)

EMPRESS: Good morning, Prime Minister. Good morning, darling. Oh! Look at you! That's a Hoot, isn't it?

EMPEROR:	It certainly is. I'm wearing it to the Grand Parade. Where have you been, darling?
EMPRESS:	Oh, just doing a little bit of shopping. I bought myself some new gowns and one of those diamond thingies and a few pairs of shoes, and guess what, darling? I got you a present. It's a lovely new tie.
EMPEROR:	Oh. Well, actually, darling, I'm fussy about ties. You know I like to choose my own, darling –
EMPRESS:	Oh, you'll love this one, darling. It's hand painted by Carlo Grotti, the tie designer. He's the name on everyone's lips, you know.
EMPEROR:	(suddenly worried) I thought Hoot was the name on everyone's lips.
EMPRESS:	Not any more, darling. It's all Grotti now. His ties are all the rage. They're terribly, terribly expensive.
EMPEROR:	Oh. Well, that's different. Let's see it, then.
EMPRESS:	(rummaging in her bags) By the way, darling, there's a tribe of grubby peasant types hanging about the gate. Waiting to see you about some fallen-down orphanage or something.
EMPEROR:	What, again? I don't know what peasants are coming to these days. Moan, moan, want this, want that. Next thing they'll be wanting to buy their own hovels. Send them home, Prime Minister, would you?
PRIME MINISTER:	Certainly, Great Noble Profileness.
EMPEROR:	And, Prime Minister? Nip along to the market and get me some lovely ribbons. Spare no expense.
PRIME MINISTER:	Right away, O Magnificent One.

(The PRIME MINISTER exits.)

EMPRESS:	Ah! Here we are!

(She fishes in her bag and produces an electrifyingly awful tie that clashes horribly with the EMPEROR's suit.)

EMPEROR: I say! <u>It is</u> rather splendid, isn't it?

EMPRESS: Try it on, darling. *(He does so.)* See how handsome you look?

EMPEROR: Mmmm. It's definitely me. But does it go with this suit?

EMPRESS: Actually, pink and tangerine do clash a bit, darling.

EMPEROR: *(wildly)* You see? Now I don't know what to wear again! Oh, bother, bother, bother!

(He throws himself into his throne and sulks. Enter the IMPERIAL MUM.)

IMPERIAL MUM: There he is! There's my big boy! Oh dear. What's this? A frown?

EMPEROR: Hello, Mumsy.

EMPRESS: He doesn't like the tie I bought him.

EMPEROR: I didn't say I didn't <u>like</u> it. It's just that a Grotti tie does not look right with this outfit, which is a Hoot! That's all.

EMPRESS: *(sniffily)* Don't wear it, then.

EMPEROR: I want to wear it, Brenda, but pink and tangerine don't go! What do you think, Mumsy?

IMPERIAL MUM: *(fondly)* I think my boy looks handsome in whatever he wears. He's a regular little smarty pants.

EMPEROR: Well, I do like to keep up with the fashions.
(He looks in the mirror and tries the tie on again. Suddenly, he is inspired.) Do you know what this tie needs? It needs a whole new outfit to set it off. Don't you think so?

EMPRESS: Absolutely, darling. You treat yourself. It's only money.

EMPEROR:	Phew! That's a weight off my mind. I'll look through all my designer catalogues and come up with something really spectacular.
IMPERIAL MUM:	That's my boy. I tell all my friends at coffee mornings. I say, if there's one thing you can be sure of about my Freddy, it's that he dresses nice.

(Lights down. ALL exit.)

Act 1, Scene 3 – Down With The Emperor!

The Market Place. We see a tableau of the FLOWER SELLER, FRUIT SELLER, RIBBON SELLER, MILKMAID, PIE MAN, BLIND BEGGAR and the SHOESHINE BOY all frozen into different positions, like statues.
The TOWNCRIERS enter at the front of the stage. One of them carries a scroll.

CRIER ONE:	Meanwhile, those crafty tricksters That we met at some time previous Have been working on a cunning plan Most devilishly devious.
CRIER TWO:	Disguised as honest weavers, They have come up with a ruse So exceptionally daring You will shiver in your shoes.
CRIER ONE:	We take you to a market place A busy, crowded street, At the centre of the city Where the common people meet.

(There is a pause.)

CRIER ONE:	Go on, then.
CRIER TWO:	That's it. I don't have another verse. Can I ring my bell instead?
CRIER ONE:	No.

(They unroll the next scroll. It reads: **DOWN WITH THE EMPEROR!***)*

CRIERS ONE & TWO: Down With The Emperor!

(They exit. The square comes to life. The TOWNSFOLK enter and mingle with the TRADESPEOPLE, examining goods and buying wares. The URCHINS run on stage and dart in and out of the crowds. The BLIND BEGGAR puts a collecting tin down on the ground beside him. The SHOESHINE BOY mimes cleaning one of the TOWNSFOLK's shoes. Everyone starts to sing the following song, to the tune of 'Frère Jacques'. It may be repeated as a round.)

WHO WILL BUY?

1. Fresh picked roses – fresh picked roses –
    Hot meat pie! Hot meat pie!
    Lovely ripe bananas, special price this morning,
    Who will buy? Who will buy?

2. Choose a ribbon for your girlfriend,
    Don't be shy, don't be shy,
    Penny for a pinta, time you had a shoe shine,
    Who will buy? Who will buy?

FLOWER SELLER: Roses! Red roses, fresh picked this morning!

MILKMAID: Milko! Penny a pint!

PIE SELLER: Pies! Hot meat pies!

RIBBON SELLER: Ribbons! Pretty ribbon for your bonnet, ma'am?

SHOESHINE BOY: Shine your shoes, sir? Only tuppence!

(A giggling URCHIN snatches the BLIND MAN's tin and runs away. The BLIND MAN runs after him.)

BLIND MAN: Oi! You bring that back, you little tyke!

FRUIT SELLER: Bananas! Lovely and ripe! Tuppence a pound!

(The BLIND MAN recovers the tin and returns to his pitch, muttering.)

BLIND MAN: Blinkin' kids!

PIE MAN: Pies! Hot pies! Who'll risk a pie?

(Enter BOGUS and FISHWEEDLE, dressed as honest weavers, carrying a loom between them.)

FISHWEEDLE: Phew! Here we are, then. The market place.
                    Right, where's the palace?

BOGUS: Patience, Fishweedle. Not so fast. We've got to get
                    established first. Get ourselves a bit of a reputation.

FISHWEEDLE: We've <u>got</u> a bit of a reputation.

BOGUS: I mean as <u>weavers</u>, Fishweedle. Things'll go a lot more
                    smoothly if the Emperor hears about our amazing skills
                    by word of mouth.

FISHWEEDLE: I'm not so sure. The scam's ready, so the sooner we...

BOGUS: Sssh!

(The PIE MAN approaches them.)

PIE MAN: *(to FISHWEEDLE)* Pies! Hot pies! Nice pie, sir?

FISHWEEDLE: What's in them?

PIE SELLER: Kind of meat.

FISHWEEDLE: What kind of meat?

PIE SELLER: Kind of rat.

FISHWEEDLE: Mmm – no thanks. Actually, we've just arrived in
                    town and we're hoping to get an audience with
                    the Emperor...

(All this time, the crowds have been bustling away in the background. At the word "Emperor", there is a gasp. Everyone whirls around and glares at FISHWEEDLE.)

SHOESHINE BOY: *(pointing)* Hear that? He said "Emperor"!

ALL: *(shaking their fists and speaking in synchronised chorus)*
<u>Down with the Emperor</u>! Boooo!

FISHWEEDLE: Sorry.

BOGUS: I take it His Majesty is not Mr Popular around here, then?

ALL: *(in chorus)* No. He's not. We think he is a mean old bat.
Don't tell him we said so.

FISHWEEDLE: Oh, that's all right. You can speak freely in front of us.
We're not exactly friends of his.

ALL: *(in chorus)* Oh. That's all right then.

(They relax and start to go about their business.)

PIE MAN: *(to FISHWEEDLE)* Sure you won't have a pie?

FISHWEEDLE: *(confidentially, to the PIE MAN)* Not just now.
You see, we're just off to the Emperor's palace to...

SHOESHINE BOY: He said it again!

(The crowd stands stock still.)

ALL: *(in chorus)* What did he say?

SHOESHINE BOY: He said "Emperor"!

ALL: *(in chorus)* <u>Down with the Emperor</u>! Boooo!

BOGUS: Yes, yes, you said that before. Look, we're just a couple of
honest weavers, off to the Emperor's palace to...

SHOESHINE BOY: They said it ag...

(FISHWEEDLE gives him a thump. The SHOESHINE BOY exits, weeping.)

BOGUS: As I was saying. We're off to the palace to make – You Know Who – an offer he can't refuse.

FRUIT SELLER: *(suspiciously)* What kind of offer?

BOGUS: All right. We'll tell you. But keep it under your hats. This is just between you, me, and the entire population of this town, right?

ALL: Right!

BOGUS: The thing is, we've developed a wonderful new fabric. We call it Polyfabuloso Cloth. Tell the people, Fishweedle.

FISHWEEDLE: Well, it's pretty amazing stuff, actually. It's a combination of the most delicate silk thread, spun gold, dewdrops picked at dawn, er... *(floundering)* star dust...

BOGUS: Mermaid hair...

FISHWEEDLE: You've never seen anything like this cloth. Such patterns! Such colours! And of course, there's its Special Magical Property.

FLOWER SELLER: Which is?

BOGUS: You really want to know?

ALL: Yes!

FISHWEEDLE: All right, then. This cloth can only be seen by the wise. To stupid people, it's <u>Totally Invisible!</u>

(Everyone registers amazement. There are lots of excited nudges and whispers.)

MILKMAID: Have you got some on you, then?

FISHWEEDLE: Certainly. Safe in the knapsack.

BLIND MAN: Let's have a look.

BOGUS: Oh, dear me, no. This stuff is unique. For the Emperor's eyes only.

ALL: (in chorus) <u>Down with the Emperor!</u> Booooo!

FRUIT SELLER: Ssssh! Here comes the Prime Minister!

ALL: (quickly, in chorus) <u>Hail to the Emperor!</u> Hooray!

(Enter the PRIME MINISTER.)

PRIME MINISTER: Out of my way at once! Where's the ribbon seller?

RIBBON SELLER: Here.

PRIME MINISTER: Right. I'll have those – and those – and three of those...

(BOGUS and FISHWEEDLE give each other a wink and put their arms around the PRIME MINISTER. They lead him off stage, talking as they go.)

BOGUS: Excuse me, sir, we couldn't help overhearing...

FISHWEEDLE: We understand you're the Emperor's most trusted minister. We've got a little proposition we'd like to put to you...

(ALL exit.)

Act 1, Scene 4 – He's Gotta Have It!

The Emperor's Chambers. The EMPEROR, wearing yet another outrageous outfit, sits on his throne with a huge catalogue on his lap, the EMPRESS files her nails, the IMPERIAL MUM knits and the FOOTMEN stand discreetly in the background.

EMPRESS: Any luck, darling?

EMPEROR: (crossly) No. (He throws down his catalogue.) Nothing's right! There's simply nothing that catches my eye. It's all dull, dull, dull. Dull and dowdy.

IMPERIAL MUM: Poor diddums. Does he want an eggy with some soldiers?

EMPEROR: Not right now, Mumsy. I'm too upset.

EMPRESS: There must be something, darling.

EMPEROR: There isn't, I tell you. It's all last year's stuff. I'm looking for something new. Something bang-up-to-the-minute. I want everyone to say, "Wow! The Emperor's really outdone himself this year." It's got to have that "Wow!" factor.

EMPRESS: And it's got to go with the tie.

EMPEROR: And look right with my crown. Oh, it's hopeless, simply hopeless! *(He stamps his foot.)* What am I going to do?

(Enter the PRIME MINISTER with a handful of ribbons.)

PRIME MINISTER: Sire! I've just got the ribbons...

EMPEROR: Yes, yes, I can see that, Prime Minister. Well, you can take them back again. I've changed my mind.

PRIME MINISTER: Ah. Well, that's all to the good, Venerable Majesty. You see, there are a couple of chaps outside that I rather think you should meet...

(Enter BOGUS and FISHWEEDLE with the loom. Pushing the PRIME MINISTER out of the way, they sweep off their hats and then they bow very low.)

BOGUS: Gracious Emperor! Bright Star Of The Firmament!

IMPERIAL MUM: Oooh! Get him!

FISHWEEDLE: We tremble in your presence, O Gorgeous One!

EMPEROR: Yes, all right, that'll do. What's all this about?

BOGUS: That's what I like. Straight to the point. We won't waste your time, sire! We are offering you the opportunity of a lifetime. The chance to be the first to model a suit made out of the new wonder material – Polyfabuloso Cloth!

EMPEROR: Polyfabuloso?

PRIME MINISTER,
EMPRESS and
IMPERIAL MUM: Polyfabuloso?

BOGUS and
FISHWEEDLE: Polyfabuloso Cloth.

(BOGUS and FISHWEEDLE sing the following song, to the tune of 'Polly Wolly Doodle'.)

POLYFABULOSO CLOTH

1.   It's the latest thing on the fashion scene,
     It's Polyfabuloso Cloth!
     It comes in red, white, blue and green
     Does Polyfabuloso Cloth,
     It's new! It's you!
     It's resistant to the moth,
     You'll look real cute in a Sunday suit made of
     Polyfabuloso Cloth!

2.   What's the latest word on every lip?
     Polyfabuloso Cloth!
     It's the happenin' thing, it's hot, it's hip,
     It's Polyfabuloso Cloth!
     Doesn't stain in the rain,
     Doesn't show spilled egg or broth,
     So have no doubt, get yourself decked out in
     Polyfabuloso Cloth!

EMPRESS: Oooh! Freddy! How exciting! I wonder if it'll go with
                     your new tie?

BOGUS: Marm, it will go with everything. And that's not all.
                     It has... *(He lowers his voice to a thrilling whisper.)*
                     Magical Properties!

IMPERIAL MUM: Oh my! Fancy! I'm coming over all funny.

EMPEROR: Magical Properties? What magical properties?

FISHWEEDLE:	Polyfabuloso, sire, is a specialist fabric. It is intended only for the eyes of the highly intelligent. People of taste. People who know True Beauty when they see it. In other words, to your average thicko, it's <u>Totally Invisible!</u>
EMPEROR:	Good heavens. Really?
EMPRESS:	Oh, Freddy. You've got to have it. You've simply got to!
EMPEROR:	What do you think, Mumsy?
IMPERIAL MUM:	My big boy's the Emperor. He can have what he wants. If he wants eggy soldiers, he can have eggy soldiers. If he wants a new suit, he can have a new suit...
EMPEROR:	Yes, all right, thank you, Mumsy. Er – is it <u>very</u> expensive?
BOGUS:	*(draws in his breath)* It'll cost you, sire. Gold thread's not cheap you know. And the magical stuff's not easy to come by. Specialist shops, you know? Pay through the earhole.
EMPEROR:	Oh, I can afford it all right. I'm rolling. And I <u>was</u> looking for something special to wear in the Grand Parade...
PRIME MINISTER:	Oh, go on, Your Majesty. Treat yourself.
EMPRESS:	Oh, do, darling. Say yes!
EMPEROR:	Well. I must admit it sounds very intriguing.
BOGUS:	Excellent! That's that then.
FISHWEEDLE:	Now all we need is the money.
EMPEROR:	Of course. See to it, would you, Prime Minister? And give them enough gold to buy whatever they need.
BOGUS:	You won't regret it, sire.

FISHWEEDLE: I think we can safely say that the sight of Your Majesty at the Grand Parade will be something the crowds will never forget!

(ALL exit.)

INTERVAL

Act 2, Scene 1 – This Is The Life!

The Weaving Room. Lights up. BOGUS and FISHWEEDLE, frozen in the act of playing cards, are sitting before the empty loom. There is a tray set with a teapot and cups and a pile of bags labelled "GOLD" sitting in the corner.

Enter the TOWNCRIERS at the front of the stage. As usual, one carries a scroll.

CRIER ONE: So. Our rogues are given money
                And then shown a private room
                Where, safe from prying eyes, they can
                Set up their stolen loom.

CRIER TWO: And then, for many nights, the pair
                Pretend that they are weaving
                When really, all they do is count
                The cash they are receiving.

(Suddenly CRIER TWO takes a trumpet from behind his back and blows it.)

CRIER ONE: What are you doing?

CRIER TWO: Blowing my own trumpet.

CRIER ONE: You just won't let it rest, will you?

*(CRIER ONE snatches the trumpet away from the crestfallen CRIER TWO. They unroll the next scroll, which reads: **THIS IS THE LIFE!**)*

CRIERS ONE & TWO: This Is The Life!

(The TOWNCRIERS exit. BOGUS and FISHWEEDLE come to life. BOGUS slams down a card.)

BOGUS: Snap! My game, I think. Any more tea in the pot, Fishweedle?

FISHWEEDLE: Nope. Time we called room service again.

BOGUS: Good idea. Ah, this is the life, eh? A roof over our heads, tea and sandwiches on tap and lots of lovely lolly rolling in.

(There is a knock at the door.)

FISHWEEDLE: Quick! You get the door. I'll get weaving.

(FISHWEEDLE pockets the cards, scurries to the loom and mimes weaving. BOGUS goes to the door. The PRIME MINISTER hovers on the threshold.)

PRIME MINISTER: Good morning, gentlemen.

BOGUS: Yes, Prime Minister? What can we do for you?

PRIME MINISTER: His Majesty is anxious to know how you're getting on.

BOGUS: Oh, fine, tell him, fine. We've been working day and night. We just need another roll of mermaid hair to finish it off.

PRIME MINISTER: Oh, right, right. I'll have the gold sent up right away. Will three bags be enough?

BOGUS: Best make it four. Just to be on the safe side.

PRIME MINISTER: Certainly, certainly. Right. Er – any chance of a peep?

BOGUS: What do you think, Fishweedle? Shall we let him?

FISHWEEDLE: I don't see why not, Bogus. After all, he got us the job.

BOGUS: You're right. Close your eyes, Prime Minister, this is your lucky day!

(The PRIME MINISTER closes his eyes. They lead him to the loom.)

BOGUS: Right. On the count of three, you can open your eyes. One – two – three!

BOTH TOGETHER: Ta da!

(The PRIME MINSTER eagerly opens his eyes, and stares at the empty loom.)

BOGUS: Isn't it grand?
FISHWEEDLE: Isn't it great?
BOGUS: Isn't it totally first rate?

FISHWEEDLE: Doesn't it gleam?
BOGUS: Doesn't it shine?
FISHWEEDLE: The fabulous hues! The clever design!

BOGUS: Look at the weave!
FISHWEEDLE: Isn't it neat?
BOGUS: Doesn't it knock you off your feet?

FISHWEEDLE: That beautiful blue –
BOGUS: That heavenly pink –

BOTH TOGETHER: So what do you think?

(The PRIME MINISTER's jaw flaps wildly.)

FISHWEEDLE: He's speechless. That's what Polyfabuloso Cloth does to people.

BOGUS: Except for the stupid ones, of course, who can't see it.

(They sigh and tap their heads pityingly.)

FISHWEEDLE: I feel sorry for them. Don't you, Prime Minister?

PRIME MINISTER: Eh? Oh – er – yes. Yes, of course. Ahem.

BOGUS: We were particularly pleased with the border. *(He points.)* See the little silver roses?

PRIME MINISTER: Oh – yes. I do, I do.

FISHWEEDLE: And the way the orange kind of merges into the buttercup yellow. See here?

PRIME MINISTER: Oh, yes. Delightful. Ha, ha, ha.

FISHWEEDLE: So you can go and tell the Emperor we're ready to take his measurements.

PRIME MINISTER: Oh. Right. Yes. Well – er – I'll go and tell him, then.

(He exits. BOGUS and FISHWEEDLE give each other the thumbs up sign. They link arms and perform a celebratory dance to a reprise of 'Polyfabuloso Cloth'.)

Act 2, Scene 2 – Time To View

The Emperor's Chambers. The EMPEROR paces up and down wearing yet another lurid ensemble. The EMPRESS sits on the throne reading 'Hello' magazine.
The IMPERIAL MUM is winding her wool, using the arms of FOOTMAN TWO.

Enter the PRIME MINISTER. The EMPEROR grabs him by the arm.

EMPEROR: Well? What happened? Did you see it?

PRIME MINISTER: I did.

EMPEROR, EMPRESS
& IMPERIAL MUM: And?

PRIME MINISTER: What can I say? It's indescribable. The way the orange sort of merges with the buttercup yellow. And the dinky little silver roses on the border.

IMPERIAL MUM: Oooh. Fancy! Roses!

EMPEROR: Really? That good, eh? You – er - didn't have any trouble <u>seeing</u> it, then?

PRIME MINISTER: Who, me? Oh, no-no-no-no-no. You forget, sire. It's only invisible to <u>stupid people</u>, ha, ha.

EMPEROR: Ha, ha. Yes, yes, of course. I was forgetting.

PRIME MINISTER: It fairly leapt off the loom at me, sire. It blazed.
It shone. It burned into my retinas. But you can see
for yourself, Your Handsomeness. They need you
to go along to be measured.

EMPRESS: Oh, goody! We can all go!

IMPERIAL MUM: Oooh, isn't it exciting!

PRIME MINISTER: I feel a little pompous parading type music is called for
here, don't you?

*(He snaps his fingers. We hear parade music. The EMPEROR and EMPRESS lead
the way off stage, followed by the IMPERIAL MUM, the PRIME MINISTER and
the FOOTMEN. This scene should flow smoothly into the next without a pause.)*

Act 2, Scene 3 – The Cloth Revealed

*The Weaving Room. As the royal procession re-enters on the other side of the stage,
BOGUS and FISHWEEDLE scurry into position at the loom.*

BOGUS: Here they come. Ready?

FISHWEEDLE: Ready.

*(FISHWEEDLE busies himself at the loom. BOGUS goes to greet the royal party.
The music fades.)*

BOGUS: *(bowing low)* Welcome, your Majesties, welcome.
This is a great moment.

EMPRESS: We're all terribly excited, Mr Bogus.

BOGUS: As well you might be. Are you ready, Mr Fishweedle?

FISHWEEDLE: I certainly am, Mr Bogus.

*(There is a drum roll from off stage. BOGUS and FISHWEEDLE stand aside and
proudly indicate the empty loom. A heavy silence falls.)*

BOGUS &
FISHWEEDLE: So what do you think?

EMPRESS: It's – it's – marvellous. Absolutely divine. I've never seen anything like it. Have you, Mumsy-In-Law?

IMPERIAL MUM: Well – no, I can't say I have.

PRIME MINISTER: *(eagerly)* You see what I mean about the roses?

EMPRESS: *(faintly)* Oh yes. You can almost smell them.

IMPERIAL MUM: Achoo! They're giving me hay fever. That's how real them roses are.

(FOOTMAN ONE hands her a hankie. She blows her nose loudly.)

BOGUS: Well, your Majesty?

FISHWEEDLE: Don't be shy.

(Slowly, the EMPEROR looks from the loom, to the audience, to his fellow actors, then back to the loom again. His face is a mask of stunned horror.)

ALL: So what do you think?

EMPEROR: But I can't ssss…

ALL: Yes?

EMPEROR: I said I can't ssss…

ALL: YES?

EMPEROR: Ahem. I can't say how delighted I am. I adore it.

ALL: He adores it!

BOGUS: Your Majesty is too kind. Come along, Fishweedle, let's roll it off the loom and take the royal measurements.

(The music for 'Polyfabuloso Cloth' strikes up again and everyone sings a reprise. As the others sing, BOGUS and FISHWEEDLE mime rolling the cloth off the loom and lowering it carefully to the floor. BOGUS takes a tape measure from around his neck and measures the EMPEROR, while FISHWEEDLE mimes jotting down the EMPEROR's measurements. The song ends.)

BOGUS: That's it, your Majesty. You can leave it to us now.

FISHWEEDLE: It'll be all ready in good time for the Grand Parade tomorrow!

(Lights down. The EMPEROR, EMPRESS, IMPERIAL MUM, PRIME MINISTER, the FOOTMEN and BOGUS and FISHWEEDLE exit.)

Act 2, Scene 4 – Ooh! He's Got No Clothes On!

The Market Place. Lights up on the TRADESPEOPLE, the BLIND BEGGAR, the SHOESHINE BOY and the TOWNSFOLK. GERT and WALTER are amongst the crowd. There is an air of excited expectancy.

Everyone sings the following song to the tune of 'She'll Be Coming Round The Mountain'.

THE GRAND PARADE

1.   All the crowds will be a-cheering when he comes,
     Yes the crowds will be a-cheering when he comes,
     We will all be busy cheering, though we really feel like jeering,
     Yes, the crowds will be a-cheering when he comes.

     Singing hip, hip, hooray for the Grand Parade,
     Singing hip, hip hooray for the Grand Parade,
     It's the high point of the year, so raise your voice and cheer,
     Singing hip, hip hooray for the Grand Parade.

(Enter the TOWNCRIERS.)

CRIER ONE: We're all here in the market place,
                     The townsfolk line the square,
                     All jostling to see what their
                     Great Emperor will wear!

CRIER TWO: They know it's very special cloth
Intended for the clever,
Each thinks – "If I can't see it,
Well, I won't admit it – <u>Ever!</u>"

(They join the crowd. Everyone sings the second verse and chorus of the song.)

2.   He will cause a huge sensation when he comes,
Yes he'll cause a huge sensation when he comes,
For the clothes he will be wearing will set the people staring,
Yes, he'll cause a huge sensation when he comes.

Singing hip, hip, hooray for the Grand Parade,
Singing hip, hip hooray for the Grand Parade,
It's the high point of the year, so raise your voice and cheer,
Singing hip, hip hooray for the Grand Parade.

(The crowd begin moaning.)

FLOWER SELLER: I dunno why we're all sounding so cheerful. It's only him showin' off again, when all's said and done.

FRUIT SELLER: You're right. It's not as if he needs any encouragement.

PIE MAN: You can say that again.

MILKMAID: Every year it's the same old thing.

RIBBON SELLER: Swaggering past us with his nose in the air.

BLIND MAN: I wouldn't have bothered to come if it wasn't for this magical cloth we've all heard so much about.

(Enter the URCHINS in great excitement.)

URCHIN ONE: The palace doors have opened!

URCHIN TWO: He's coming!

URCHIN THREE: Old Snooty's on his way!

BLIND MAN: Get out of the way, I can't see a blinkin' thing!

(The parade music strikes up again. To loud cheers, the procession slowly makes its way on to the stage. First the FOOTMEN, followed by BOGUS and FISHWEEDLE, the PRIME MINISTER, the EMPRESS, the IMPERIAL MUM – and lastly, the EMPEROR. He is wearing his crown, Grotti tie, a large pair of spotty boxer shorts and a patronising smile. He waves languidly to his public and halts centre stage. The music fades. The cheers slowly die away. There is a long pause. A sudden cry breaks the silence.)

SHOESHINE BOY: Ooooh! He's got no clothes on!

(There is a gasp, a couple of seconds of silence, then the laughter begins. The noise gradually rises in volume until everybody, apart from the royal party, is helpless with mirth. BOGUS and FISHWEEDLE, realising the game is up, hastily tiptoe off stage. Realisation slowly dawns on the EMPEROR. With a look of fury, he turns to the PRIME MINISTER, who whips off his cloak, covers the EMPEROR as best he can, and bundles him off stage. They are quickly followed off stage by the FOOTMEN, the EMPRESS and the IMPERIAL MUM.)

IMPERIAL MUM: Freddy! Mummy's got a hankie! Come to Mummy, there's a good boy…

(Everyone is still laughing. They link arms and sing the last verse and chorus of the song.)

3.   Well, you saw what he was wearing when he came,
       Yes you saw what he was wearing when he came,
       We all stood about and laughed because he looked so flippin' daft,
       And we somehow think he'll never be the same.

       Singing hip, hip, hooray for the Grand Parade,
       Singing hip, hip hooray for the Grand Parade,
       It's the high point of the year, so raise your voice and cheer,
       Singing hip, hip hooray for the Grand Parade.

(Everyone except the TOWNCRIERS exit, singing the last chorus as they go. The TOWNCRIERS are left alone.)

CRIER ONE: This is it, isn't it? End of the story.

CRIER TWO: 'Fraid so.

CRIER ONE: I suppose we ought to tie up the loose ends.

CRIER TWO: Like what?

CRIER ONE: Well – what happened to Bogus and Fishweedle,
for a start.

CRIER TWO: Funnily enough, I got a postcard from them this
morning. From Spain. *(He takes a postcard from his
pocket and reads it.)* "Having a lovely time. Sorry we
had to rush off. Keep the loom as a momento. We've
retired. Love, Bogus and Fishweedle." No forwarding
address, of course. Nice of them, though, wasn't it?

CRIER ONE: Very nice. So I guess you could say they lived happily
ever after.

CRIER TWO: I'd say it was very likely. I don't know about
the Emperor, though. Do you?

CRIER ONE: Well, you know, I heard a rumour that he'd changed
his ways. Became more humble. Bought himself
a sensible coat and a flat cap. Fixed up the drains.
Rebuilt the orphanage. Started a workers co-operative.

CRIER TWO: Well, well. That makes a very satisfactory ending,
I think. Shall we wind it up?

CRIER ONE: Let's.

CRIERS ONE & TWO: We hope you have enjoyed our play.
We thank you, one and all.
Please put your hands together
For the final curtain call –

CRIERS ONE & TWO: And, finally, remember
As you wend your way home sadly,
<u>Do not put pink with tangerine.</u>
<u>It clashes really badly!</u>

(To loud, cheerful music, the entire cast come on stage and take their bows. The EMPEROR enters, wearing a long dark overcoat and cloth cap, and walks to the front of the stage. He waits for the applause to subside. The music fades.)

EMPEROR: *(to the audience)* So what do you think?

(Another pause. He looks down at himself.)

EMPEROR: Nah.

(He whips off the overcoat. Underneath, he is wearing the most outrageous outfit seen so far. FOOTMAN ONE removes his cap, FOOTMAN TWO places an immensely tall crown on his head. The EMPEROR is himself once more. The entire cast could sing a favourite song as a finale.)

(The TOWNCRIERS move centre stage and ceremoniously unroll their last scroll. It reads – **THE END**.*)*

THE END

Staging

Area for Performance

You will need to stage *The Emperor's New Clothes* to fit the space you are using. You may have a hall with a fixed stage or rostra blocks, or you may simply be using the space at the front of a classroom.

If you have a hall with a fixed stage, keep the sets as simple as possible to avoid scene-changing delays. If your stage has curtains, these can be closed between scenes. The Towncriers can perform the Prologue and the introductions to Act 1, scene 2, Act 1, scene 3, and Act 2, scene 1 in front of the curtains, while the scene is changed behind them. Rostra blocks can be used to extend an existing stage and create a more flexible space.

If you have no stage but do have rostra blocks, you can use them to create a stage on different levels with different areas for each location. The arrangement shown in the diagram has the advantage that the Market Place and the Emperor's Chambers can stay in the same place throughout the play. Only one area has to double up – as the Weaving Room and the Wood. Scenery and props are quite easy to move, so this shouldn't be a problem.

Backdrops

Backdrops are certainly not essential. An actor can simply hold out a sign from the wings, which says, for example, **The Emperor's Chambers**. This is an easy way to indicate a location.

On the other hand, making a backdrop is an activity that lots of children might enjoy. Before you embark on backdrops, first make sure you have somewhere to hang or display them. Work out how large the backdrop will need to be and construct it by sticking together large sheets of paper with masking tape. Sketch out the scene on the front and then paint it or decorate it with a collage. Although it is possible to create a different backdrop for each of the four main locations, you might prefer to create a single, all-purpose backdrop, which could show timbered houses with the palace in the background.

Scenery and Props

You can make the scenery and props as simple or as elaborate as you wish. Here are a few ideas to help you:

The Wood

The only essential large props are a tree stump which the characters sit on and a tree for them to hide behind. The tree stump can be made from a low stool and a large piece of cardboard. Cut a tree trunk shape that will completely hide the stool. Paint the shape. Attach the tree trunk shape to the front of the stool. If you haven't got time to make a cardboard cut-out tree, you could use an artificial Christmas tree instead.

The Emperor's Chambers

The focal point of this set will be a splendid throne. A full-size upright chair with arms is best for this. Create a large back for the chair from cardboard and decorate it lavishly. Tape string to the back of the cardboard shape. Tie it to the back of the chair. Use brightly coloured crepe paper to conceal the lower part of the chair. Use tinsel for further decoration if you like.

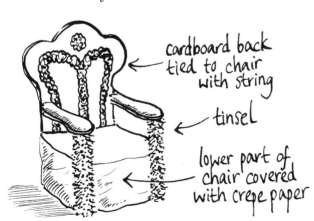

You will also need a coat stand to display the Emperor's red and blue outfits, which are not worn. Other outlandish cloaks, scarves and hats can be draped over the stand.

The Emperor needs a mirror to pose in front of. It should be positioned so that the Emperor is still easily visible to the audience when he looks at himself in it, as shown in this bird's eye view.

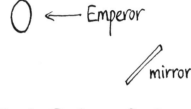

To make the mirror, you will need a large rectangular piece of cardboard. Stick a smaller rectangle of silver foil to the front. Paint the back to match the frame.

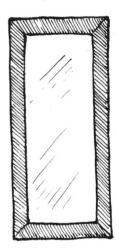

To make a stand to support the mirror, use a piece of strong cardboard about as long as the mirror is high. Paint it to match. Cut it into the shape shown here and fold it along the dotted lines.

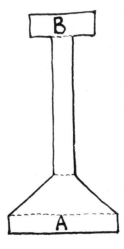

To fix the support to the mirror, fix flap A at the base and flap B slightly higher than halfway up the mirror. Make sure your mirror is standing at the right angle before you glue flap B into place.

Scenery and Props

The Market Place
You will need to keep this set as clear as possible to accommodate the large number of actors in these scenes.

The Weaving Room
The only essential props are some sacks of gold. These can be made from bin bags filled with scrunched-up balls of paper. The sacks should be clearly labelled 'GOLD'!

You could supply chairs for Bogus and Fishweedle and an orange box for them to play cards on as well.

Alternatively, they may sit cross-legged on the floor. You will need a small table or covered box to support the loom (see page 39 overleaf for an explanation of how to make the loom.)

Props

There are a number of small props required for each scene. It is a good idea to set up a props table backstage from which the actors collect their own props.

Prologue
A megaphone for Crier One
A bell and piece of paper for Crier Two
Scrolls for the Criers (Prologue, Act 1, sc. 2, Act 1, sc. 3, Act 2, sc. 1, Act 2, sc. 4 and a postcard for the last scene.)
Act 1, scene 1
An apple for Gert
A basket with washing, whistle, rattle and hooter in it for Gert
An axe for Walter
Act 1, scene 2
Shopping bags with an orange tie inside for the Empress
Act 1, scene 3
A collecting tin for the Blind Beggar
A fruit tray for the Fruit Seller
A ribbon tray for the Ribbon Seller
A pie tray for the Pieman
A jug for the Milkmaid
A loom for Bogus and Fishweedle (also in all their scenes in Act 2)
Act 1, scene 4
A catalogue for the Emperor
A nail file for the Empress
Knitting for the Imperial Mum
Ribbons for the Prime Minister
Act 2, scene 1
A toy trumpet for Crier Two
Playing cards for Bogus and Fishweedle
A tray set with teapot and cups
Act 2, scene 2
Hello! magazine for the Empress
Act 2, scene 3
A hankie for Footman One
A tape measure for Bogus

Scenery and Props

Some of these props are easy to find, but others may need to be made. Here are some suggestions to help you.

A Loom

A large rectangular cardboard box with the sides cut down to 8cm in height makes a good base for the loom. String the loom evenly with lengths of strong thread, as shown.

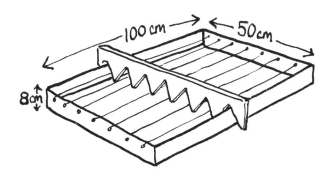

Use Foamcore or a strip of cardboard from the left over box to make an arm for the loom. The loom arm should be 56cm wide (slightly wider than the loom itself) and 10cm deep. Make the loom arm's teeth evenly spaced and 7cm deep.

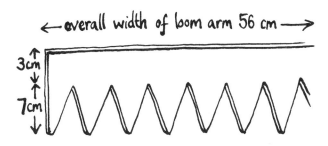

Five Scrolls

The Towncriers need five A3 scrolls. The scrolls should be clearly labelled as follows: THE EMPEROR'S NEW CLOTHES, TALK ABOUT VAIN!, DOWN WITH THE EMPEROR!, THIS IS THE LIFE!, THE END. They can be rolled up and attached with a piece of Blu-Tack for easy unfurling.

An Axe

This can be quite simply constructed out of a single stout piece of cardboard. Paint the handle brown and use silver foil or paint to cover the blade.

Tradespeople's Trays

You can make trays for ribbons, pies, flowers and fruit. Cut down a smallish cardboard box so it has a rim about 6cm high. Paint the outside. Make two holes through each of the short sides of the box and thread ribbon through them to hang around the actor's neck. Adjust the length of the ribbon for each person.

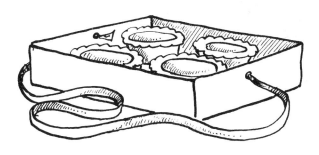

The **Flower Seller**'s tray could contain tissue paper flowers. For each flower you will need a long strip of tissue paper about 8cm wide. Make deep snips all along one edge. Roll the paper up (with the strips you have cut at the top.) Fasten the roll at the bottom to make the flower's stem. Gently spread out the strips at the top to make the petals.
The **Ribbon Seller**'s tray can contain strips of material and some real ribbons for the Prime Minister to buy.
The **Fruit Seller**'s tray could contain painted fruit made from modelling clay. Glue the fruit to the base of the tray.
The **Pie Man**'s pies could be made from white paper party bowls with cardboard tops glued on. Decorate the tops to look like pastry. Fix the pies to the tray.

Lighting

If you are using hired lighting, this will be supervised by an adult. If you are using ceiling lights, someone could be given the job of turning them on and off at the right times.

Lights may be turned off during scene changes. Also, you may choose moments during the play when it would be effective to turn them off and on again.

For instance, at the very end of the play when the cast have taken their bows, the lights could be switched off and then turned on again for the Emperor to step forward with his last lines.

Casting and Auditions

Choosing your Cast

First hold a meeting and tell everyone the story of the play. Talk to them about the main characters in the play, using the illustrations on pages 42 – 43 to help you. Discuss the area you are going to use for the play and how you intend to stage it. It might be interesting to find out if any of the children have ever been to the theatre and what they remember about it.

At this stage it's not a bad idea to talk a little about life in a real theatre and explain that there are many crucial roles apart from those which involve acting. Describe all work which goes on behind the scenes including stage management, costume, scenery, props and music. Make it clear from the start that every aspect of the production is important. Explain that taking on a big acting role means spending a lot of time learning lines and taking direction. It is not for the faint-hearted!

At this point some of the children will gravitate away from acting, so let them know that you will soon be making decisions about scenery painters, stage managers, musicians and dancers. You will find that you will be able to include everybody who wants to take an active part in the production.

Casting and Auditions

The Auditions

Those of you who are new to auditioning may find the following drama exercises useful. They are designed to help you explore the natural acting talents of your cast.

• Choose a scene from the play. Act 1, scene 3, which takes place in the busy Market Place would be a possible choice. Ask the children to close their eyes and listen carefully while you describe the characters and action in that scene. Help each child to choose a character (such as a trader, beggar, or urchin) and explain that, at a given signal, they are to grow into their characters and improvise an activity that they think they might perform during the scene.

• Divide the children into pairs and ask each pair to improvise a scene between the Emperor (or Empress) and a servant. The Emperor is deciding what to wear and is giving the servant a very hard time. Give them plenty of time to work out the scene and explore their characters before they show it to you.

• Divide the children into groups of five

or six. Tell them to pretend they are at a Towncriers' convention. Within each group they all have to take turns to stand up and tell a joke in their best Towncrier manner.

• Divide the children into groups of three. Ask each group to improvise a scene in the Weaving Room between Bogus, Fishweedle and the Emperor. While the scoundrels pretend to weave and describe the beauties of their "cloth", the Emperor will be trying hard not to show that he can't see it.

By the end of this session, you will have a good idea which children can really concentrate on this sort of activity, and show the ability to immerse themselves in a role.

The next stage is to distribute the scripts for a "read through" the following day. At the read through allow each child to read different parts before you make your final decisions.

If you have a great many more children than you have parts, remember that there are no limits to the numbers of Townsfolk and Urchins you can have.

The Main Characters

The Towncriers
Possessed of big voices and a rather oddball sense of humour.

Bogus and Fishweedle
Likeable villains with a smooth line in chat.

Gert the Washerwoman
A kindly sort, but a bit slow on the uptake.

Walter the Woodcutter
Grouchy, stubborn and very, very dim.

The Footmen
Always poker-faced. They never register any emotion.

The Imperial Mum
A highly-coloured pantomime
dame type. She treats the
Emperor like a little boy.

The Empress
Spoilt, empty-headed
and generally
rather silly.

The Prime Minister
Grovellingly servile.

The Emperor
Vain, self-obsessed,
petulant and selfish.

The Stage Management Team

You will need about eight (or more) children in the stage management team. They can all be given individual tasks. Its a good idea to involve all the children in the team in rehearsals from the beginning. This means everyone will be aware of what they're doing by the time of the final performance.

Scene Shifters
Two or more children could be in charge of carrying large props and pieces of scenery on and off and changing the backdrops, if necessary.

Lighting
If you hire lighting, you will need an adult to supervise its use. If you are using ceiling lights only, one child could be given the job of switching them on and off as required. He or she will also need a playscript marked with the lighting cues.

Props Table
You will need two organised individuals to be responsible for the props table. They need to check that personal props are on the table for the actors to collect before they go on stage.

Director's Assistant
This job calls for a helpful, reliable individual to take messages, make lists, remember things and bring you cups of tea as required!

Prompter
One alert member of the team can act as prompter. He or she should be seated inconspicuously with a copy of the playscript, ready to remind the actors of their lines.

Sound Effects
There are only a few sound effects in the play, so this job only requires one capable person, who could also be in charge of tape recorded music. He or she will need a playscript marked with the sound effects and music cues.

Rehearsal Schedule

You will need to consult with other members of staff over the vital question of rehearsal times. For instance, will all rehearsals take place at lunch time or can some time be set aside during school hours?

Plan each rehearsal carefully, to keep numbers to a minimum, so that you won't have some children hanging around with nothing to do. The dates for the final run through and dress rehearsal need to be decided early on.

Costume

Although some schools are fortunate enough to have good costume wardrobes, others may not. Luckily, the costumes for this play can be devised quite simply from very basic materials. The following suggestions are divided into Male, Female and Unisex roles, but feel free to adapt them to suit your particular cast.

Male Roles

The Emperor

The Emperor requires several costumes. He will need at least two different outfits for his first three scenes, one of which would be his pink Hoot suit. In his fourth appearance he wears only a pair of ridiculous boxer shorts and a silly tie. For his final appearance he wears a cloth cap and a dark overcoat on top of the silliest costume of all. You can make the Emperor's costumes as zany as you wish, adapting the text if necessary.

One possibility would be to use a variety of brightly coloured shirts and leggings in different clashing combinations. The leggings can be rolled up to the knee and worn over a pair of tights. Gold ribbon or tinsel could be worn at the knees and wrists. The Emperor could wear an elaborate cloak too (see page 46).

The Emperor will also need two crowns. The first crown can be fairly traditional, but the second crown should be very tall and quite absurd. A traditional crown can be made from card, cotton wool and crepe paper. Use a strip of card about 6cm wide to make the headband.

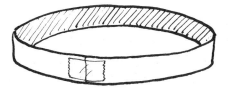

Cut two strips of gold card about 3cm thick and 50cm long to make the top of the crown. Bend the strips across each other and tape the ends to the inside of the headband.

Next, push a piece of crepe paper (it should be pink or orange rather than red) into the crown and tape it in place. Glue cotton wool from a roll around the outside of the headband and dot with black felt pen to make it look like ermine.

The second crown could be made from gold card rolled to fit the actor's head. (A piece of elastic might be needed under the chin.) This could be decorated with pieces of tinsel.

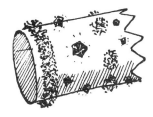

Costume

Male Roles

The Prime Minister
A sober jacket and trousers would be ideal for this part. Remember that he needs a coat or cloak to cover the Emperor with in the last scene of the play.

Bogus and Fishweedle
These actors will both need two costumes. They first appear in their convicts' suits. Use grey or black tracksuits or striped pyjamas. Stick the lettering "PRISON PROPERTY" across their chests. They will each need a ball and chain. The balls can be made from papier-mâché. Paste the papier-mâché over a balloon to create your ball. (The balloon can be burst when the papier-mâché is dry.) Paint them grey. Attach them with paper chains.

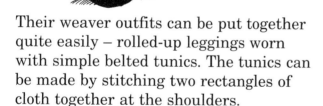

Their weaver outfits can be put together quite easily – rolled-up leggings worn with simple belted tunics. The tunics can be made by stitching two rectangles of cloth together at the shoulders.

Walter the Woodman
He can wear tracksuit bottoms stuffed into wellington boots, topped with a belted tunic. Create a beard with face paints.

The Footmen
They each need a wig. You can make one from a double sheet of a newspaper. Fold it in half length-ways. Repeat the folding twice more. Then cut the strip as shown, making the cuts 4cm apart. Unfold it carefully.

Female Roles

The Empress
An old bridesmaid's dress or cut-down evening dress would be ideal for the Empress. Add lots of jewellery, and make up her face. You could make her a royal cloak from bin bags and cotton wool. First make a neckband by rolling one bin bag up along its length until it is about 5cm wide. Tape the ends of other bin bags to the neckband so they all overlap at the top. As you tape the bin bags together, let them flare out towards the bottom. If the cloak is too short, add another layer of bin liners. Glue strips of cotton wool on to the cloak for fur and dot it with a black pen to make it look like ermine. Attach a piece of string or ribbon under one end of the neckband and make a hole at the other end of the neckband, so that you can fasten the cloak.

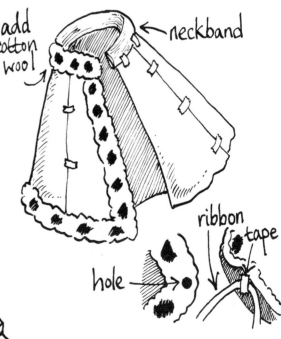

Gert the Washerwoman
Gert needs a simple frock and an apron with clothes pegs pinned around it. She could wear a simple headscarf.

Costume

The Tradespeople

Female Tradespeople

The **Ribbon Seller**, **Fruit Seller**, **Flower Seller** and **Milkmaid** can all wear costumes made quite simply from a leotard and two skirts. One skirt is used as the underskirt and the other as the overskirt. The overskirt is bunched up and pinned to the underskirt with safety pins covered with bows. They could wear headscarves too.

Male Tradespeople

The **Pie Man** can wear leggings and a plain top. He will need a simple cook's hat. Make this in the same way as the Emperor's first crown, using a white card headband and two crossbands. Push white crepe paper inside them to make the top of the hat.

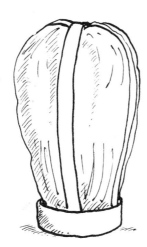

The **Shoeshine Boy** could wear a flat cap and a ragged shirt and trousers. He could have a brush and duster.
The **Blind Beggar** could wear an old overcoat, a floppy hat and dark glasses. He could carry a white cane.

Unisex Roles

The Imperial Mum
In the tradition of the pantomime dame, this part can be played by a boy. His/her costume and make up should as be over-the-top as possible. He/she could wear a brightly coloured dress and a flamboyant crown similar to the Emperor's tall crown. Curling ringlets made from gift-wrapping ribbon could be hung from it.

His/her knitting bag contains giant needles and a long multi-coloured scarf.

The Urchins
The boys can wear trousers or leggings with simple shirts and caps and the girls skirts and shawls. Tack on patches to make their clothes look worn. Smear their legs with black face paint to make them look dirty. They can all go barefoot.

The Townsfolk
Their costumes should be as varied as possible and can be designed to use the clothes you have available. Some can be dressed as country farmers or peasants, wearing smocks and straw hats. Others could be respectable couples out for a stroll. There could be a teacher with a class of children or a nanny with a pram. Some characters should have baskets to put their purchases in. One or two might carry milk jugs.

Music

There are four original songs in the play which have all been written so that they can be sung to well-known tunes. Generally, the actors on stage are required to sing the songs while remaining in character. It's a good idea to use a choir or chorus as well. This will take the pressure off the actors and allow more children to be involved. The accompaniment could be provided by piano, percussion, recorders or by a full orchestra – whatever suits the talents you have available.

The script calls for "Pompous Parade type music" on two occasions. Something like Haydn's Trumpet Voluntary would be very suitable.

Dances

There is only one dance suggested in the script, at the end of Act 2, scene 1. It is a dance of celebration performed by Bogus and Fishweedle to the song 'Polyfabuloso Cloth'. The two actors should stand close together or link arms and jig from side to side and then backwards and forwards, clapping or slapping their knees as well. This dance calls for plenty of silliness!

There is room to accommodate more children in another dance in Act 1, scene 3, which takes place after the song 'Who Will Buy?' You can arrange it to suit your production, but a country dance or folk dance might work well.

Sound Effects

The sound effects can be achieved as follows:

Walter's axe cutting through the chain = strike the rim of a drum.

A knock at the door = rap a block of wood on a table top.

A drum roll = play two drums simultaneously.

Anything Else?

However frazzled you may be feeling as the big day approaches, try not to lose your enthusiasm – keep calm and keep smiling if you can! Don't worry if the dress rehearsal doesn't run smoothly. Children usually reserve their best performances for the real thing, and it will all be all right on the night!

One final project might be to create a simple programme, using the children's own illustrations. This would list all the children who have contributed to the production and would enable you to thank others who have helped along the way.

Enjoy yourselves!